GREAT BIG TRAIN

For Nico

GREAT BIG TRAIN
A RED FOX BOOK 978 0 099 45597 4

First published in Great Britain by Hutchinson,
an imprint of Random House Children's Publishers UK
A Random House Group Company

Hutchinson edition published as *The Great Big Little Red Train* 2003
Red Fox edition published as *The Great Big Little Red Train* 2004
Red Fox edition re-issued 2009

11

Red Fox Books are published by Random House Children's Publishers UK
61–63 Uxbridge Road, London W5 5SA

www.randomhousechildrens.co.uk

Addresses for companies within The Random House Group Limited can be found at:
www.randomhouse.co.uk/offices.htm

THE RANDOM HOUSE GROUP Limited Reg. No. 954009

A CIP catalogue record for this book is available from the British Library.

Printed in China

LITTLE RED TRAIN

GREAT BIG TRAIN

Benedict Blathwayt

RED FOX

Duffy and Jack were sitting in Jack's guard's van having a quiet cup of tea when a large lorry drove past the railway sidings.

"Haven't you got any work to do, mate?" the lorry driver yelled at Duffy. "I'm not surprised. A train that old and small is no use to anyone! It belongs in a museum; or on the scrap heap."

Surely the Little Red Train doesn't look that old and useless, thought Duffy.

Just then Duffy and Jack had three unexpected visitors.

"The furniture for my autumn sale is stuck at the docks," said the showroom manager.

"I want gravel from the quarry for my concrete mixers," grumbled the cement works foreman.

"I need to collect timber from the forest," said the sawmill owner.

"Why aren't the lorries delivering by road as usual?" Duffy asked his visitors.

"Terrible traffic," they groaned, "roadworks, breakdowns, faulty traffic lights. We were wondering if the Little Red Train could help us. The old track and trucks are still there somewhere."

"We'll see what we can do,"
said Duffy.
"Don't forget the oil can, Jack!"

The Little Red Train set off at top speed.
Clicketty clack, clicketty clack
Clicketty clicketty clicketty clack

SLOW

"I can see why the lorries aren't getting anywhere,"
Duffy called out to Jack in the guard's van.

When the Little Red Train reached the docks, Duffy and Jack
kept a look out for the old railway sidings.

"Here they are!" yelled Jack, jumping down to oil the points.
"And there are plenty of old trucks too."

Duffy hitched up the trucks to the Little Red Train with
Jack's van at the back.

The old railway line led right along
the dockside and under a huge crane.

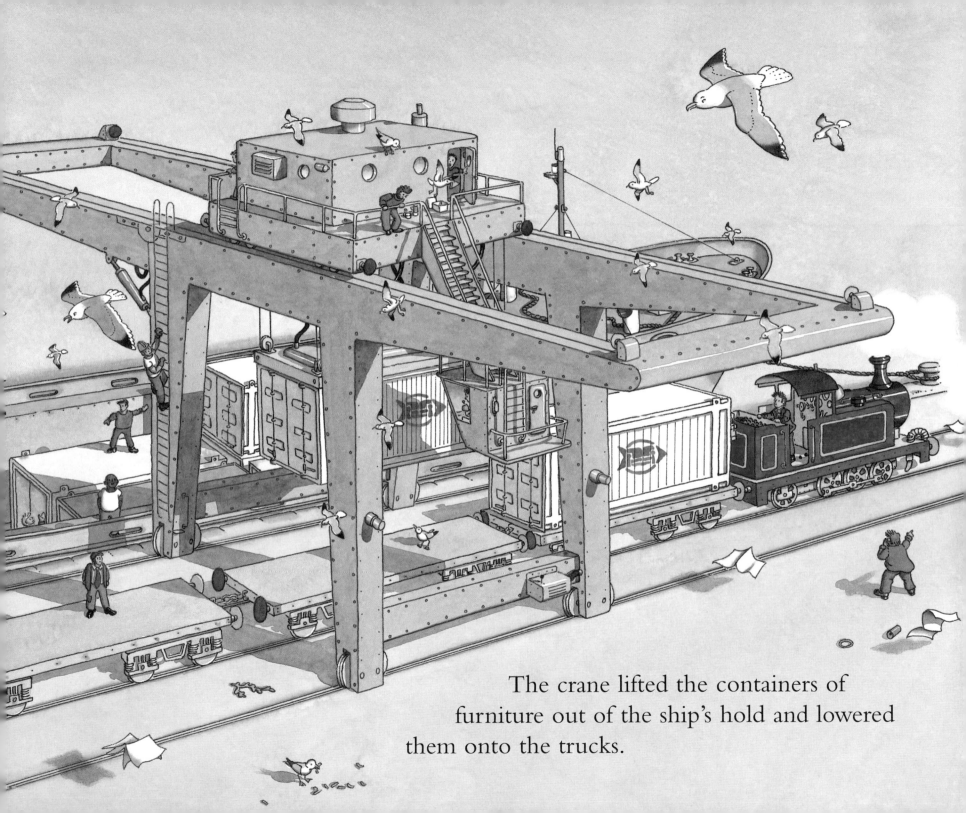

The crane lifted the containers of furniture out of the ship's hold and lowered them onto the trucks.

When all the trucks were loaded,
the Little Red Train steamed out of the
old sidings and back onto the main line.
"Off to the quarry now," said Duffy.
Huff-chuff . . . huff-chuff . . . huff-chuff went
the steam from the Little Red Train's pistons.
Creak . . . squeak went the rusty wheels on
the trucks. *Cree . . . eak, squee . . . eeak*

When they arrived at the quarry the old railway line
was almost completely hidden under a layer of dust.
   "There are a lot of old gravel trucks here," said Jack.
"Let's hitch them up at the front."

One by one the quarry hopper
filled the trucks with gravel.

"Off to the forest now," said Duffy. "I hope the Little Red Train is strong enough to pull all these trucks."

Huffitty-chuffitty . . . huffitty-chuffitty . . . huffitty-chuffitty puff went the smoke from the Little Red Train's funnel.

Creak . . . screech went the truck wheels on the rusty track. *Cree . . . ee . . . eak, scree . . . ee . . . eech*

When they arrived at the forest, Duffy and Jack soon found the overgrown tracks and some flatbed trucks hidden in the brambles. Duffy guided the Little Red Train onto the old tracks and hooked up the trucks at the front.

The foresters loaded lots of long logs onto
the trucks and they were ready to go.
"Let's head for home!" said Duffy.

The Little Red Train's wheels spun, and smoke and steam
puffed furiously from its funnel.

Huffitty-puffitty . . . huffitty-puffitty . . . huffitty-puffitty puff

Very, very slowly the long chain of trucks – with the
tree trunks from the forest, the gravel from the quarry
and the furniture from the docks – followed the Little
Red Train out onto the main line.

And right at the back of the very, very long train
came Jack's guard's van.

Whoo . . . ooo . . . eee whistled the great big Little
Red Train.

Duffy waved to the lorry drivers who were still stuck in a traffic jam.

When Duffy and Jack arrived home the showroom manager and the cement works boss and the sawmill owner were ready to help them unload. "Thank goodness for the Little Red Train," they said. "We'd have been stuck without you!"

Duffy and Jack cleaned and oiled the trucks.
And then they gave the Little Red Train a
shiny new coat of paint.

"We're ready for our next job now," said
Duffy proudly. "Well done, Little Red Train."

More exciting stories to enjoy!

Picture Story Books

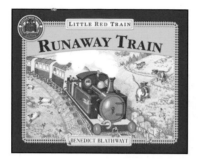

(also available as a Story Book and CD)

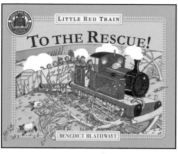

(also available as a Story Book and CD)

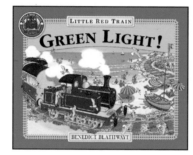

(also available as a Story Book and CD)

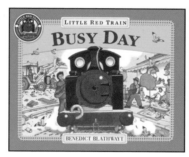

(also available as a Story Book and CD)

(also available as a Story Book and CD)

(also available as a Story Book and CD)

Gift Books

Stop That Train! – A Pop-Through-the-Slot Book

Little Red Train Adventure Playset

The Runaway Train Pop-up Book

The Runaway Train Sticker Frieze

The Little Red Train Gift Collection

The Runaway Train Book and DVD